About the Author

Steven Dale has been happily married for 38 years. He has two daughters and three granddaughters. He currently lives in Alicante, Spain where he until recently, worked as a Vocal Entertainer. He's now retired from singing and concentrates all his efforts on writing. *The Planet Mirth Adventures One* is his first children's book.

Dedication

For my granddaughters Niamh,
Mia and Miriam.

Steven Dale

The Planet Mirth Adventures One

AUSTIN MACAULEY PUBLISHERS™

LONDON • CAMBRIDGE • NEW YORK • SHARJAH

ISBN 9781786294470 (Paperback)
ISBN 9781786294487 (Hardback)
ISBN 9781786294494 (E-Book)
www.austinmacauley.com

First Published (2017)
Austin Macauley Publishers ™ Ltd
25 Canada Square
Canary Wharf
London
E14 5LQ

CONTENTS

The Safari

"Look Mammy! It's the Planet Mirth and it looks just like home," said Mia as she looked out of the spaceship window.

She was six years old and this was her first trip into space. They had just landed after a yearlong journey from Earth.

"Are there animals here like we have back home?" she asked.
"Yes Mia, but they're different. Everything is different."
"What do you mean Mammy?"

"You'll find out tomorrow, when we go on safari. Everything you see will make you happy. That's what Mirth means: happiness and enjoyment. No one cries here, unless they're tears of laughter," said her mother as they walked through the tunnel into the airport.

"What's that Mum? It looks like a television but it's wobbly," she asked.

"It's a jellyvision. A lot of things are made of jelly on Mirth. There's even a jellycopter."

"That's so cool," she said as she laughed.

"That's nothing. Wait until you see the humans," said her mother.

As they walked through, they were met by a man with two heads. Both heads were sucking on a lollipop.

"My name is Ping," said the first head.

"And my name is Pong," said the second head.

"Welcome to," said Ping. "The Planet Mirth," said Pong.

"Your transport is ready and waiting," they both said together, as they led them outside.

"Wow! He's got two heads Mum," she said amazed.

"They say two heads are better than one. If they have a problem, they've got two brains to work it out," replied her mother as they stepped through the airport doors.

"What is that Mum?" she asked as she stared at the odd looking creature with the head of a horse and the body of a rhinoceros.

"It's called a rhinhorseros. He'll be taking us to our hotel." Ping and Pong, helped them aboard and then tied their suitcases to the back.

Mia enjoyed the journey and was even more amazed when the rhinhorseros began to talk. "My name is Ros," he said. He told them all about the planet, and named all the plants that grew on the roadside.

"That one there, the tall one, is called a Bunflower. When it grows big, you can pick the bread buns and eat them. The one next to it is a Hambush. You can pick the ham and put it in your bun. That one there is a daftodill. When it flowers in spring, it laughs and giggles all day."

When they arrived at the hotel, they were welcomed by a team of gnomes who ran around excitedly. One of the gnomes stood on the shoulders of another, then pulled the suitcases down from the back of the rhinhorseros, and carried them into the hotel.

As Mia and her mother walked through the entrance, all the gnomes began to sing their welcome song.

WE WELCOME YOU BOTH TO THE PLANET CALLED MIRTH
WHERE PEOPLE DON'T CRY LIKE THEY DO ON EARTH
WHERE CHOCOLATE IS FREE TO GOOD GIRLS AND BOYS
AND THINGS GROW ON TREES, ESPECIALLY TOYS.

"Chocolate is free and toys grow on trees? What does that mean Mammy?" she asked.

"You'll find out tomorrow, when we go on safari," replied her mother.

The following morning, they both sat in the restaurant eating their breakfast. They were served by a very tall man who had spaghetti growing on his head, instead of hair.

"Why have you got spaghetti growing on your head?" asked Mia, frowning.

"I like it. When I'm hungry I just help myself," he replied.
"This place is crazy," she said to her mother.

"I know. Now eat your breakfast. Ros is waiting for us."

After breakfast, they both climbed on board and set off on safari.

"Good morning!" said Ros happily. "I'll be taking you to the magical forest today. On the way, you'll see all sorts of animals and flowers. If you have any questions, just ask."

After a few minutes, Mia spotted an animal that looked like an elephant, but had a tree and some bushes growing on his back.

"What is that Ros?" she asked.

"It's an eleplant. He grows his own food on his back," he replied.

"What about that one over there? It looks like a donkey but it's only got three legs."

"That's a wonkey."

Mia sat in silence for a while, enjoying the view. Fields of different coloured grass stretched for miles, every colour you could imagine. They eventually arrived at the entrance to the magical forest, where Ros stopped for them to climb off.

"There's a stream over there where you can have a drink before you enter the forest," he said.

Mia approached the stream with her mother, then had the fright of her life.

"There's a crocodile!" she screamed.

"That's not a crocodile. It's a chocodile. He's made of chocolate," said her mother laughing.

"He's got bars of chocolate growing on his back!" shouted Mia. "That's special chocolate. If you've been a good girl, you can break the chocolate off and eat it. If you've been naughty, it won't work."

"How do you know all these things Mammy?" she asked.
"I came here when I was a little girl," she replied as Mia bent down and reached out for some chocolate. It broke off easily into her hand.

"Yes! I've been a good girl!" she shouted.

After a drink of water, they entered the forest where Mia had the surprise of her life. All around her, toys hung from the trees. Every toy you could possibly imagine was there. A doll hung above her head, one she'd always wanted.

"You told me toys don't grow on trees Mammy," she said.

"That's on Earth, but they do here," she replied.

"Can I pick it off?" she asked her mum.

"Yes. But it will only come off if you've been a good girl. It won't work for naughty children, just like the chocolate."

She reached up and pulled the doll. It came off easily into her hand.

"Yes! I've been a good girl," she screamed with delight.

"That's why it's important to be a good girl. On Earth, Santa only brings toys to good girls and boys. Mia! Mia! Mia! Wake up! Your breakfast is ready!"

Mia opened her eyes and then realised she'd been dreaming. She was back on Earth, in her own bed and her mother stood in front of her with a smile on her face.

"I had the strangest dream Mammy. I was on the Planet Mirth and chocolate and toys were free," she said.

"I had a dream like that when I was a little girl. Now get dressed, it's time for school," said her mother.

THE
BURPDAY

"I wonder if I'll dream of the Planet Mirth tonight Mammy?" said Mia as her mother tucked her into bed.

"I'm sure you will," she replied as she began to read her a bedtime story. Five minutes later, Mia drifted off to sleep, only to be awoken by a squeaky voice.

"Wake up! Wake up! It's a very special Mirthday. One of the gnomes is having a Burpday!"

She opened her eyes to find her mother standing by her bed.

"Was that you who spoke Mammy?" she asked curiously.

"No Mia. That was your pillow," she replied.

"Don't be silly Mammy. Pillows don't talk." she said.

"Your pillow does. It's actually a sheep with a pillow growing on his back," replied her mother.

"But it's pink. Sheep are normally white," said Mia.

"Sheep can be any colour on Mirth, depending on what colour grass they eat. If they eat pink grass, they'll have pink wool."

"Wow! That's cool. Do they always wake up the children in the morning?" she asked.

"No. Not always. Only on special occasions," replied her mother. "What's a burpday?" she asked.

"When a gnome does his first burp, his family remember the day and celebrate it every year. It's Jerome the gnome's 10th burpday today and they're having a party in the field across the road. It starts at breakfast time and goes on all day," said her mother.

"Do the gnomes have sheep pillows to wake them up?" she asked.

"No Mia. They use an alarm sock. When it's time to get up, a stinky smelly sock drops from the ceiling and lands on their nose. The smell wakes them up," said her mother.

"Grampa's socks would wake them up. They're really smelly," said Mia, chuckling to herself.

"Well get dressed Mia or we'll miss the fun. I've got an invitation here for the two of us and I don't want to be late," she said. "Yippee!" shouted Mia as she jumped out of bed.

"I've got a present here for you to give Jerome," said her mother as she handed her a parcel wrapped in gold paper. "What is it Mum?" she asked.

"It's a pair of grampa's stinky socks," she replied. "Good idea Mum. He'll love them," said Mia as she tied her shoelaces.

"We'll have to take our invitation to the penguins first, so they can tick the box with a pen," said her mother as they walked out of the lift.

Mia was amazed. They were surrounded by gnomes who had travelled there from all over the planet. They were all waving their invitations in the air as they looked around for a penguin. "Wow! Jerome has a lot of friends," said Mia.

"That's because he's polite and always shares his sweets, but they're also here for the Mirth Games that start in two days time," said her mother.

"There's a penguin Mum and he's got a pen growing out of his face where his nose should be!" she shouted.

"That's why they call them penguins Mia. They write books all day for the chickens to read," said her mother.

"Chickens read? Are you sure Mammy?" she asked.

"Yes. I'll show you on the way to the field," replied her mum. Mia handed the invitation to the penguin who bowed politely and ticked the box on the bottom.

"Have a nice day Mia," he said as he gave it back to her.

When they got outside, they saw Ros who had ten gnomes on his back.

"Good morning to you both," he said as the gnomes slid down his tail and ran into the hotel.

"Be careful crossing the road Mia and make sure you use the zebra. There's a lot of traffic today," he said.
"Thank you. I will," she replied.

On the way, they stopped off at the chicken shed to see the chickens reading.

Mia was astonished. All of them wore strange looking glasses and were lined up on shelves with books in front of them.

"Their glasses are not very nice Mammy," she said with a frown.

"Maybe they should have gone to Pecsavers," replied her mother giggling.

"Do they speak?" she asked.

"Only one word and that's 'book'. If they haven't got one they go mad and shout 'book book book' all day, until somebody gives them one," replied her mother.

"This planet's crazy Mum," she said as they walked through the door and headed for the field.

As they neared the main road, they could see miles of rhinhorseroses, all queuing to get into the hotel car park.

"Look Mum. There's a giraffe with lights on his neck, by the side of the road," Mia said excitedly.

"That's a giraffic light and he's controlling the traffic. It's exactly like a traffic light on Earth," she said.

"And look! There's a zebra with a pole growing out of his head. It's like a big lollipop stick."

"That's the zebra crossing of course," said her mother.
They waited on the pavement until the zebra said it was safe to cross, then entered the field.

Hundreds of gnomes sat around tables that covered the whole area, except for the middle where a giant bouncy castle stood.

"Please and Thank You are very unusual names," said Mia.
"It's to make sure everyone remembers their manners," said her mother.

The grass shoppers returned with the meals and placed them on the table.

"Thank you, Please," said Mia to the first one.

"Thank you, Thank You," said her mother to the second one.

They both cleared their plates, enjoying every mouthful when a trumpet sounded, making them jump with surprise.

"What's that for Mum?" she shouted with alarm.

"They're bringing out Jerome's burpday cake," said her mother.

Mia looked up and saw the biggest cake she had ever seen in her life. It was the size of a house and had wheels underneath it. Ros was pulling it along.

Ping and Pong sat on top of the cake, cutting off slices and throwing them at the gnomes.

"Look out!" shouted Mia as a piece of cake flew through the air and hit her mother straight in the face. She looked at her mother and laughed as another piece landed on her head. Within minutes, there was a big cake fight, with gnomes grabbing handfuls and throwing them at each other.

"Do they always do this?" asked Mia.

"Yes, but only on burpdays," replied her mother.

A few minutes later, another trumpet sounded, ending the cake fight. Mia and her mum were in tears of laughter. The best fun they'd had in ages.

Everything went quiet as a smaller cake was wheeled in, with ten candles burning brightly on top. They stopped in front of Jerome, who stood up and began to breathe in and out in a strange way.

"What's he doing Mum?" she asked.

"He's getting ready to burp. It's got to be a big one. Enough to blow the candles out," said her mother.

"That's not very good manners," she said.

"You're right Mia. If you have to burp, you should put your hand over your mouth," said her mother as Jerome burped loudly, blowing out the candles.

All the gnomes cheered loudly and began to sing the burpday song.

"Happy burpday to you. Happy burpday to you. Your burps are smelly, they're from your belly. Happy burpday to you."

As the song ended, Mia could feel herself drifting off to sleep, with her head resting on the table. She woke up to her mother's familiar voice. "Wake up Mia! It's time for school."

THE MIRTH GAMES

Two days later, Mia rushed home from school, excited. She changed into her pyjamas, sat on the sofa and waited patiently for bedtime.

"You're dressed early," said her mother surprised.

"It's the Mirth Games today and I don't want to miss anything," she replied.

By 7.30 she was tucked up in bed, while her mother read her a bedtime story. Within seconds she drifted off, only to be awoken by a sharp knock on the door. As she opened her eyes she realised she was back on Mirth with her mother standing by her bed.

"Message for Mia!" came a voice from behind the door.

"Who would have a message for me?" she asked.

"It's probably a mobile gnome. They deliver all the messages on Mirth," replied her mother.

Mia opened the door to find a worried looking gnome standing there.

"An urgent message from Ming the King of the gnomes. He's just arrived to open the games and would like to speak to you downstairs," he said.

"I wonder what he wants?" said Mia, concerned.

"You'd better get dressed so we can find out," replied her mother.

They arrived downstairs to a room full of gnomes. One of them looked different to the others. He had two extra eyes on the back of his head and walked backwards.

"Why is he walking like that?" she asked her mother curiously.

"He's from the planet Stupiter where they all walk backwards and he's here for the backwards race. They've won it every year since the games began.

"The Planet Stupiter? Where is that?" she asked.

"Not far from here. About an hour by spaceship," replied her mother.

"Ah Mia. I've been looking for you. Ming the King wants to speak to you," said Jerome as he hobbled towards them on crutches.

"What happened to you?" asked Mia, concerned.

"I broke my ankle on my burpday. I slipped on a piece of cake and went flying. Come quick. The king is waiting!" he shouted as he led them to a room at the back.

As they entered the room, a trumpet sounded making them both Jump. A gnome with a long grey beard announced their arrival.

"Mia and her mother to see the King!" he shouted as he led them to a big golden chair where the king sat.

"Ah Mia! At last," said Ming. "We need your help. Jerome the gnome was supposed to run in the backwards race but he's broken his ankle. Will you run in his place? None of the other gnomes want to do it."

"But I'm not a gnome," said Mia.

"It doesn't matter. We've checked the rules and as long as you're under four foot tall you can run," he said as the gnome with the long grey beard approached Mia with a four foot stick, and held it against her.

"She's under four foot!" he shouted as a cheer went up in the room.

"Then it's settled. Mia will run. Now let's go and open these games," said the King as he rose from his chair.

"I've never run in a race before Mum. I'm nervous," said Mia as they walked to the field.

"Just do your best. It's the taking part that's important, not the winning," she replied.

As they sat down at a table, another trumpet sounded.

"Silence for the king!" announced the bearded gnome.
The whole field went quiet as the king began to speak.

"I, Ming the King, want the games to begin," he announced as the crowd went wild with excitement. "The first game shall be the high jump!"

Mia and her mother walked over to the high jump area to watch them warming up. Her jaw dropped open when she saw the strange looking creatures that were taking part. They had the body of a man from the waist up, but their bottom half was Kangaroo.

"What are they called?" she asked.

"Mankaroos. They can jump as high as a house. The record is twenty feet," replied her mother.

They began to jump over a high wall but after an hour, there were only two left in the competition. With the wall set at twenty-one feet, the first one began his run. He took off and flew through the air like a bird but as he came down, his foot caught the wall, setting off an alarm. The crowd cheered him even though he'd failed.

The second one began his run and flew through the air like a spaceship. He cleared the wall by an inch, setting a new Mirth record. The crowd went mad, cheering and shouting.

The king approached him and placed a gold medal around his neck. The Mankaroo hopped away, waving his arms in the air with delight.

"Come on Mia. The piggy back race is about to start," said her mother as they walked to another part of the field.

"We've done that in school. You have to carry someone on your back," said Mia.

"This game is different. The gnomes have to ride pigs that are a little bit bigger than the ones on Earth."

"That sounds like fun," said Mia as the race started.

Ten pigs raced off, with their gnomes holding on tight. After ten yards, two of them fell off and slid across the mud towards Mia. The others raced on towards the finishing line. The winner was the gnome with the long grey beard. The king presented him with his medal as the crowd cheered.

"Your race is about to start Mia. You'd better go to the starting line," said Jerome as he limped towards them.

"Don't forget Mia. It's two laps of the field, so don't use all your energy up at the beginning and check your laces. Make sure they're done up tight," said her mother as Mia took her place at the starting line.

She checked her laces as the king began to speak to the crowd.

"A special welcome to Mia who's running in the backwards race for the first time!" he yelled as the crowd began to shout her name.

MIA MIA DO YOUR BEST. RUN LIKE THE WIND
AND BEAT THE REST.
MIA MIA DO YOUR BEST. RUN LIKE THE WIND
AND BEAT THE REST.

"Ready! Steady! Go!" yelled the king.

They all began to race as fast as they could but Mia took her time and stayed at the back. Two of the gnomes tripped over each other and had to drop out of the race, leaving only four left in.

After the first lap, Mia was in last place but getting closer to the others. With half a lap left, she began to pass them as the gnomes began to get tired.

As they neared the finishing line, there was only one gnome in front of her who was from the planet Stupiter. It looked as if he was going to win, but there was one important thing that he'd forgotten to check. His laces.

Three steps from the line, he stepped on one of them and went tumbling through the air as Mia overtook him to win the race.

The crowd went crazy with excitement, jumping with joy and kissing each other.

The king approached Mia and placed the gold medal around her neck.

"Well done Mia. We're all proud of you," he said as the crowd shouted her name over and over.

MIA! MIA! MIA! WAKE UP! YOUR BREAKFAST IS READY!

51

HALLOWEEN

Mia returned home from a Halloween party at her friend's house, dressed as a witch. She changed quickly into her pyjamas and ran up to bed.

"I wonder if I'll dream of Mirth tonight. I haven't been there for ages," she said as her mother tucked her in.

"Maybe you will," replied her mother as Mia drifted off to sleep.

A few minutes later, her sheep pillow woke her up.

"WAKE UP MIA! THERE'S THINGS TO BE SEEN! THE WITCHES ARE COMING. IT'S HALLOWEEN!"

She looked around and then realised where she was.

"What witches are coming?" she asked her mother who was stood by her bed.

"The witch tree witches from the magical forest. They look after the sweets that grow on the witch trees. There's one there especially for you and all the sweets on it are yours," replied her mother.

"How will I know which witch tree is mine?" she asked.

"You'll find out later," replied her mother.

"What do they look like Mum? Are they good or are they bad?" she asked excitedly.

"There are no bad witches on Mirth, only good ones. They have green hair, green skin, a hooked nose with a wart on the end that looks like a Rice Krispie and knees that wobble when they walk," she replied.

"When are we going to see them?" she asked.

"Now, Mia. As soon as you're dressed. They'll be arriving soon."

"But it's morning! I thought witches only come out at night, when it's dark." said Mia.

"But this is Mirth. It's dark all day on Halloween," replied her mother.

When they got downstairs, they met Ping and Pong, the man with two heads.

"Hello, hello," they both said together. "There's a fireworks display later," said Ping. "And we have magic fireworks," said Pong. "Come and join us. We'll have loads of fun," they both said together.

"We'd love to. Thank you for inviting us," said Mia, remembering her manners.

When they got outside, they saw hundreds of children from Earth, all walking towards the field with their parents.

They crossed the road by the zebra and entered the field. A big bonfire burnt brightly in the middle. Another area had been prepared for fireworks with a big fence around it.

"Remember Mia. You must stay behind the fence for safety.

Only Ping and Pong are allowed to light the fireworks," said her mother.

"OK Mum, I'll remember, but where are the witches?" she asked.

"They'll be arriving over there any minute," replied her mother, pointing to a road made of sponge. "That's Broomstick Airport. It's made of sponge so they don't hurt themselves when they land."

"There they are!" she shouted as she looked up.

Hundreds of witches on broomsticks filled the sky and began to land, one by one. When the last one had landed, they all stood together and began to sing to the children and their parents.

WE ARE THE WITCHES THAT WATCH THE WITCH TREES.
WE ARE THE WITCHES WITH WOBBLY KNEES.

WHICH WITCH TREE IS YOURS, WE HEAR YOU ALL SAY.
JUST JUMP ON OUR BROOMSTICKS, THEY'LL SHOW
YOU THE WAY.

When they had finished singing, one of the witches stepped forward and began to speak to them.

"My name is Winnie The Witch. You are going to have a broomstick race to the magical forest, where you will find your tree. The first one there will win a prize. The broomstick knows which tree is yours, so just hold on tight and enjoy the ride. One adult and one child must ride together, but remember, there's no steering wheel. You only have to think of a word and the broomstick will read your mind. If you think of the word fast, it will go fast and if you think of the word slow, it will go slow and so on."

"I think this is going to be fun," said Mia as a witch handed her a broomstick.

Her mother climbed on first, then Mia clung on behind her.

"There's no seatbelt," said Mia, as a seatbelt clicked around her waist.

"You thought of the word seatbelt so one appeared," replied her mother.

"Everybody get ready. ONE, TWO, THREE. FLY TO YOUR TREE!" yelled Winnie as the race began.

Her mother shouted the word fly and the broomstick took off into the air. Some of the other families were still on the ground and hadn't thought of the word.

"Faster!" shouted her mother as the broomstick shot ahead of the others.

After a few minutes, Mia could see a big wall in front of them, blocking the way.

"There's a tunnel! We have to fly through it!" she yelled.

"Down! Down!" shouted her mother as they entered the tunnel and flew straight through.

When they came out the other side it was raining.

"Umbrella!" shouted her mother as one appeared above them and kept them dry.

A few minutes later they arrived at her tree, a long time before the others.

"We've won! We've won!" yelled Mia with delight. "I wonder what the prize is?"

"You're good at driving a broomstick Mum," said Mia.

"That's because I've done it before. I entered the race with your grandmother when I was a little girl. We came second,"

she replied as a witch approached them carrying a small box wrapped in gold paper.

"This is your prize," she said as she handed it to Mia.

She opened it carefully, taking care not to drop it.

"It's a music box," Mia said with delight.

"Not just a music box, but a magic one. If you place it by your bed, every Saturday, your favourite bar of chocolate will appear inside," said the witch.

"Wow! That's awesome!" said Mia.

"It's time to pick the sweets from your tree. You have to get back in time for the fireworks," said the witch as she handed her a bucket.

Within minutes her bucket was full, leaving plenty left on the tree.

"What will happen to the sweets that are left? Can you send them to the poor children on Earth?" she asked.

"Of course we can Mia. I'll see to it straight away. Now fly back as quick as you can or you'll miss the fireworks."

They arrived back safely, landing on the sponge road as the witches cheered loudly.

"Well done you two," said Winnie as the first firework shot into the air, lighting up the sky behind them.

"Thank you. It was great fun," they both replied together, as they walked towards the fence by the fireworks display.

When they got there, Ping and Pong were waiting with a firework in their hands.

"This one is especially for you Mia. You have to write your name on the side of it," they said.

She did as she was told and handed it back.

A few minutes later, the firework took off and her name appeared in the sky in beautiful colours.

"Look! It says

Mia! Mia! Mia!

Wake up! It's Saturday and there's a parcel here from grandmother."

Mia jumped out of bed. She was back on Earth. She opened the parcel and was amazed to see the music box with her favourite bar of chocolate inside.

THE MIRTHMAS DINNER

It was Christmas Eve on Earth and Mia was excited. She laid her stocking down on the floor outside her bedroom door and jumped into bed. Her mother began to read "T'was The Night Before Christmas", her favourite story and within minutes she was asleep.

Her sheep pillow woke her up singing a familiar song but the words were different.

JINGLE BELLS, JINGLE BELLS, IT'S MIRTHMAS DAY TODAY. A SPECIAL MEAL FOR YOU TO EAT AND LOADS OF GAMES TO PLAY.

"Come on Mia. Get dressed. We've been invited to the gnomes Mirthmas dinner," said her mother.

She jumped out of bed, dressed and then looked out of her

bedroom window at the field opposite.

"Look Mum! There's hundreds of snowmen out there. They're alive and carrying big boxes."

"That's because they're delivering carrots for the gnomes' dinner. They grow them up in the mountains and this time of year they give them away, but they keep their best one to use as a nose."

"What time is the dinner Mum?"

"It won't be long, just after the sprout eating competition." "Yuck! I don't fancy that," said Mia with a disgusted look on her face.

They hurried downstairs into a full restaurant and sat at a table with Jerome. A mountain of sprouts were piled high in the middle of the room, surrounded by gnomes who were tucking in.

Some of them had fallen asleep, too full to eat anymore.

After a while, there were only two gnomes left eating. When they reached one hundred sprouts, the whole room began to sing and cheer them on.

"ONE MORE SPROUT, IN YOUR BIG BELLY, BUT DON'T BREAK WIND, BECAUSE YOU'LL BE SMELLY!"

Finally, one of them collapsed onto the mountain of sprouts, but as he fell he broke wind and took off like a rocket. He flew straight through an open window into the field opposite.

The other gnomes cheered and laughed as the king placed a medal around the winner's neck. A gold sprout on a gold chain.

"Do you have toys on Mirthmas like we do on Earth?" Mia asked Jerome.

"Of course we do. We pick them off the trees, but we are only allowed five. The rest of them are sent to Santa Claus on Earth and he takes them to the good girls and boys."

"How do they grow?" asked Mia.

"Every time a child does a kind thing on Earth, a toy grows. Do you remember on Halloween when you asked for your sweets to be sent to the poor children?"
"Yes. There were too many for me."

"Well that day, a lot of toys grew because you'd done a kind thing," said Jerome as a waiter placed a dish of carrot soup in front of him.
"That looks nice," said Mia.

"We have to use up the carrots. We have soup first followed by roast carrots then carrot cake for dessert."

"What will I have?" she asked as the waiter gave her an empty dish.
"That's a magic dish. Just close your eyes and wish for whatever food you want," said Jerome.

"Wow!" said Mia as she closed her eyes and wished.

Her favourite meal, spaghetti bolognese appeared before her.
"This is great," she said, licking her lips.
Later on she wished for apple tart and custard and ate it all.
"Now it's time for fun and games," said Jerome as two gnomes wheeled a big machine into the room.
"What's that?" she asked.

"It's a bubble machine!" yelled Jerome with delight. "My favourite game."

74

"What's a bubble machine?" asked Mia.

"Have you ever blown bubbles with soapy water when you're on Earth?" he asked.

"Yes. But we don't use a big machine like that."

"This machine makes giant bubbles. If you stand in the middle, the bubble surrounds you, then you can float around the room. It's great fun but it only lasts about a minute, then the bubble drops to the floor and pops."

"I want to try it," she said excitedly.

"Well come on then. Let's join the queue," he replied.

They waited patiently as other gnomes took off and floated around the room. Eventually it was her turn. She stepped into the machine and stood there nervously as a bubble formed around her and floated off. A few times she fell over, but after a while she found her balance. She floated for a while as she waved to her mother and the other gnomes.

A minute later, she landed on the sprouts, sending them flying.

"That was great fun," she said to her mother. "Can I go again?"

"Of course Mia. Enjoy yourself. It's Mirthmas day," she replied. She did it a few times on her own, then tried it with Jerome. They both floated off together but it didn't last as long, because they were too heavy.

"We'd better sit down Mia because Ming the King is about to start the custard fight," said Jerome as the waiters placed a plate of custard in front of everyone.

"That sounds fun," said Mia, remembering the cake fight on Jerome's burpday.

The king stood up with a plate of custard in his hand and began to speak.

"Now it's time for the custard fight!" he screamed as he looked at the gnome sitting next to him, and slapped the plate straight into his face.

The whole room went crazy. Mia's mother sneaked up behind her, tapped her on the shoulder and pushed a full plate of custard into her face.

Mia laughed loudly, as she did the same to Jerome.

There was custard everywhere with everyone slipping and sliding around the floor.

Fresh plates of custard were brought in by the waiters as the gnomes threw them at each other.

The king sneaked up on Mia with a plateful, but as he got close, she spotted him and grabbed his hands and pushed the plate into his face.

"Well done Mia," he said laughing. "You got me with my own plate."

A few minutes later, they ran out of custard and the game ended. Mia sat next to her mother, exhausted.

"This has been one of the best days ever Mum." she said

"It certainly has, especially the magic dish. I wish we had them on Earth so I wouldn't have to worry about cooking Christmas dinner Mia, Mia! Mia! Wake up! It's Christmas!"

Mia opened her eyes, jumped out of bed and got her stocking. "Santa's been!" she yelled as she opened her presents. "Merry Mirthmas Mum. No, I mean Christmas."